WARTON'S CHRISTMAS EVE ADVENTURE

THIS BOOK BELONGS TO

amy Capron

OTHER YEARLING BOOKS YOU WILL ENJOY:

WARTON'S CHRISTMAS EVE ADVENTURE

by RUSSELL E. ERICKSON

pictures by
LAWRENCE DI FIORI

A YEARLING BOOK

A YEARLING BOOK
Published by
Dell Publishing Co., Inc.
1 Dag Hammarskjold Plaza
New York, New York 10017

Yearling® TM 913705, Dell Publishing Co., Inc.

ISBN: 0-440-49068-5

Reprinted by arrangement with William Morrow & Company, Inc.

Printed in the United States of America

First Yearling printing — October 1979

CW

WARTON'S CHRISTMAS EVE ADVENTURE

Nearly all the signs of winter were upon the deep forest. The days were short, the nights were long. Little streams bubbled over icy stones, and chill winds swept down from the high mountains. The only sign still missing, although it was nearly Christmas, was snow. That is what Warton the toad was discussing with his brother Morton, one dark night.

Outside it was bitter cold, but, in their home deep in the ground, it was cozy and warm. Warton was up on a stepladder, adjusting the glittery star that topped their Christmas tree. "I know you don't care much for snow," he shouted to his brother, "but it won't seem like Christmas without it."

"I suppose that's true," answered Morton from the kitchen, where he was busy with his holiday cooking.

Warton climbed down off the stepladder. He looked at the gaily wrapped packages under the tree. Then he picked up a square box wrapped in green paper and yellow ribbon. A little tag on it read:

To Morton From Guess Who?

Warton could hardly wait to see the look on his brother's face when he opened the box on Christmas Eve and discovered the one thing he had been wanting for so long — a spaghetti-making machine.

Putting the box back, Warton noticed a small package wrapped in red paper. Its tag said:

To Warton —
Positively Do Not Open Till Christmas!

Warton shook it carefully, and felt something heavy inside slide back and forth. "Oh, oh," he said. "This could be the jackknife I've been wanting — the one with seven blades plus

a fork and spoon. He put it back and went into the kitchen.

The air in the kitchen was filled with the aroma of freshly baked pastries. Pies and cakes sat cooling on the countertop.. On the table were platters piled high with cookies and candies. Warton breathed deeply of the mouth-watering smells, then sat down in the rocking chair next to the stove, and sighed.

"Don't you have anything to do?" asked Morton as he sifted a cup of flour.

"Not a thing," replied Warton. "I've already cleaned and polished everything three times, the tree is decorated, and all the packages are wrapped, and yet, Christmas Eve isn't until tomorrow night. I just know tomorrow is going to be the longest day in the whole year."

"Well, it won't be long enough for me," said Morton, wiping flour from his nose. For me it's cooking, and more cooking."

"Would you like some help?" asked Warton hopefully.

"Of course not," said Morton. "You know I work best alone. And, since Grampa Arbuckle is bringing his old friend Sebastian the field mouse this year, I want everything to be perfect. Although I'm wondering if a field mouse will like my usual Christmas Eve dinner."

Warton looked aghast. "Morton!" he cried. "How could anyone not like your Christmas Eve dinner? Why, wait till Sebastian tastes your waterbug soup; it's so delicate and delicious. And wait till he sees Grampa Arbuckle carve the roast jumbo crayfish, all golden brown and filled with your special moth egg stuffing. And think of mashed potato bugs with gravy and creamed clover mites!" Warton

12

smacked his lips. "And all that, topped off with a slice of white fly pie and a cup of elderberry tea. I can't imagine *anyone* not loving such a meal."

"I hope you're right," said Morton.

"I'm sure I am," said Warton. "And now I'm even more certain that tomorrow's going to be a very long day."

As Morton began cracking walnuts with a wooden mallet, Warton leaned back and closed his eyes. Slowly, he began to blink — one eye at

a time. It was something he always did when he thought really hard. His eyes blinked faster and faster, and then stopped.

"I have it!" he shouted, jumping out of the rocker. "The perfect way to make time fly tomorrow!"

"And what might that be?" asked Morton cautiously. He had learned long ago that some of Warton's ideas could be rather startling and, sometimes, even dangerous.

"Well," said Warton, just as his brother was about to strike a walnut, "tomorrow I am going to go . . . ice-skating!"

Morton's eyes popped open. The mallet flew into the air, and disappeared into a pan of gingerbread batter.

"Don't you think it's a good idea?" said Warton.

"A good idea?" choked Morton. "It's a terrible idea. Toads were meant to stay underground in the winter . . . and under snow . . . and under everything. We were meant to stay where it's warm and cozy and . . . safe."

14

"But there is no snow," said Warton. "And I have plenty of warm clothes, and the ice must be very thick by now, and . . ."

Morton let him say no more. "I can see your mind's made up," he said, "and I certainly can't blame you for wanting tomorrow to pass quickly. But, tell me, how can you go ice-skating if you don't have ice skates?"

Warton grinned. "I'm going to make some," he said, "this very night. And, because of you, I know exactly how to do it."

First, Warton took a pair of old hiking boots that were firm around the ankles. Then he hopped over to the table where Morton had been opening walnuts. He picked out two pieces of shell with hard, sharp edges. He carved and shaped and sanded and rubbed them till they were perfectly sharp. Finally, he put just the right curves to the tips, and fastened them to the boots.

"There," he said with satisfaction, "tomorrow I'll be gliding over that ice faster than the wind itself."

Morton just shook his head and went to bed.

The first thing the next morning, Warton washed and dressed quickly. He put on his warm knickers, his bright, argyle socks, his blue, quilted jacket, insulated with milkweed down, his knitted cap, and his red earmuffs.

Warton tiptoed past Morton's door and into the kitchen. But Morton was already at work. The sink was filled with dishes, and the top

of the stove seemed alive with pots and pans that puffed and steamed and bubbled and hissed. Morton was dashing back and forth, and looked as happy as could be.

Warton, eager to be off, gulped down a tall glass of sparkling crab apple juice, and quickly ate a big helping of scrambled grasshopper eggs and three mushroom muffins.

"There," said Warton, wiping a bit of egg from the corner of his mouth, "I'm ready for skating."

"Then take this with you," said Morton, handing him a small pack. "I've put in a thermos of hot chocolate and some assorted Christmas cookies."

"Thank you," said Warton. "I just wish you were coming along for the fun, Morton." Then he opened the door, and stepped into the tunnel that led to the out-of-doors.

"And remember," Morton called, "be careful."

"Don't worry," said Warton. Then he made his way up to the forest floor.

He was glad he had dressed warmly, for the air was cold. The pale blue sky was filling with milky clouds, and the winter sun seemed to hold no heat at all. As he hurried along the path, Warton noticed the stillness of the forest. Except for the shriek of a blue jay, there was only the sound of his own footsteps on the frozen earth.

The path he traveled was wide and clear most of the way, but narrowed now and then as it passed behind boulders or curved around fallen logs.

After a while Warton came to the top of an open hillside. The grass that had once grown green and thick now lay brown and bent. At the bottom of the frozen hillside was the pond. Instead of being blue, and sparkling in the sun as he had imagined, it was dark and looked like a huge piece of gray slate.

Warton hurried along. Halfway down the hillside he came to a stone wall. He was about to climb over it when he heard, "Oh Drat!"

Then came a thud and a bump, a crash and a

clattering. Then all was silence. Next, an alarm clock began to ring.

Warton scrambled to the top of the wall and cautiously peered over it. He saw a small red wagon lying upside down. Next to the wagon, sitting on the ground and rubbing his head, was a little mole. He was so bundled up that only his tiny black eyes showed above his muffler. Scattered all over the ground were packages and boxes and clothing. There was also an alarm clock and a small, somewhat bedraggled Christmas tree.

"What happened? Are you all right?" called Warton.

The mole blinked and looked around. "Oh hello, Sir, wherever you are. My name's Monroe and I'm fine, thank you. How are you?" The mole smiled as he waited for an answer.

Warton hopped down off the wall. "I'm fine too," he said, "and my name's Warton."

"Oh," said the mole. Then he grinned. "I'm afraid I don't see too well in bright daylight. That's why I didn't see you . . . and whoever ran into me."

"I think it was this stone wall," said Warton. "Would you like me to help you reload your wagon?"

"That would be a great help," said the mole. "Then I would get to my sister Matilda's home even sooner. Every year I visit her and my twenty-three nephews and nieces for the holidays, and I always bring the Christmas tree."

Warton and Monroe turned the wagon right side up, reloaded the mole's belongings, and tied the Christmas tree on top.

"Will you be all right now?" asked Warton.

"Oh, yes," replied the mole, "Matilda lives right at the top of this hillside." He took his wagon by the handle and started off up the hill. "Merry Christmas, Warton," he called.

"Merry Christmas," answered Warton, continuing on his way. The closer he got to the pond, the more excited he became. By the time he reached the bottom of the hill, he was running.

Suddenly, there it was. It gave him a strange feeling to know that, beneath all that ice, there was nothing but deep, dark, cold water. Cautiously, Warton crept a short way from the edge. He held his breath and jumped into the air. When he landed, the ice felt as solid as if it were his own floor back home. Satisfied that the ice was safe, Warton sat down and quickly

put on his skates. As soon as he stood up, his legs crossed, and down he fell.

"Hmm," said Warton, "I'd better take this pack off before there is nothing left but cookie crumbs." He set it on a tree stump which was sticking up through the ice.

The next time he tried skating, his legs shot out from under him, and down he fell again.

After ten more falls, Warton finally made both legs go in the same direction at the same time. Soon he was taking longer and longer strides. Then he began to make curves and turns, and, by noontime, he was skating all over the pond. Then Warton decided it was time for hot chocolate so he sat down on the stump, and took out his thermos.

"As soon as I'm finished," he thought, "I'll work on figure eights."

He was taking his first sip of hot chocolate when he felt something wet on his nose. He crossed his eyes to see what it was. On the very end of his nose sat a perfectly formed, pure white snowflake.

"It's snowing!" cried Warton happily. He watched with fascination as the flakes fluttered about him. After a while, he decided he had better return home. He put on his pack, skated to the edge of the pond, and removed his skates.

As he climbed the hillside, he thought of the fun he had had ice-skating. "If I could only get Morton to try it," he thought.

Then suddenly, he heard, "Oh Drat! Drat! Drat! How can something be so hard to find? I know it's here somewhere."

Warton peered through the snow, and made out a little bundled-up figure, scurrying about. "It's Monroe the mole!" he thought. "What happened, Monroe?" he called. "I thought you were going straight to your sister's home."

The mole squinted. "Oh, hello, Warton," he said. "My muffler made my nose itch and, when I sneezed, my wagon rolled away. I've been trying to find it ever since."

"Perhaps I can help you," offered Warton.

"Oh no," said Monroe, "you should be get-

24

ting home yourself. If you wait much longer, it will be too late."

The snow was driving hard now, and it stung Warton's face. He knew he ought to go home, but he knew there was little chance that Monroe would find the wagon by himself. And he could imagine how much the Christmas tree meant to the twenty-three little moles.

"We'll find it!" he cried. He started hopping about, searching everywhere. All the time the snow was falling faster and faster, becoming more difficult to walk through. Warton sat on a mound of snow to catch his breath. The

moment he did, an alarm clock began to ring.

"Monroe!" shouted Warton. "I've found your wagon!"

"That's wonderful!" answered Monroe from somewhere in the swirling snow. "Now, keep on making noise so I can find *you*."

"All right," answered Warton. He decided that this was a perfect time to do something he had always wanted to do—yodel in a snow storm. He took a deep breath and began. He was concentrating very hard, when something poked him.

"Warton," came Monroe's muffled voice, "are you gargling?"

"I'm yodeling," said Warton. "Now look, here's your wagon."

"What a relief," sighed Monroe. "Thanks to you, those children will have their Christmas tree."

"I'm very glad," said Warton. "But now I must hurry home."

As Monroe waved goodbye, Warton hurried off. He went a short way and then stopped. He made a small turn, took a few steps and stopped again. Shielding his eyes against the blinding snow, he looked in every direction. He spun around once, and then twice. A lump formed in his throat, and a chill ran up his back. "I'm lost!" he cried.

Instantly, thoughts of home rushed into his head. At that moment, he knew, Morton was bustling about, trying to finish all his cooking. Soon it would be time to go next door to Grampa Arbuckle's to sing carols around the old player piano. Later, back at Warton and Morton's home they would sit down to the Christmas Eve feast. And, after that, it would be time to open presents. And then, at midnight, there would come his favorite part of Christmas Eve—

"I must try to find my way home," he said firmly. And he struck out through the snow. He trudged steadily along until an object appeared just before him. It was Monroe again, pulling his wagon and whistling a little song.

"Monroe!" cried Warton.

"Warton!" gasped Monroe. "What are you doing here? I thought you went home."

"I can't find my way," said Warton.

Monroe stood directly in front of Warton and shouted as a gust of wind blew in his face, "Then you must come with me to my sister's home! You can stay as long as you want!"

"Thank you," said Warton, relieved at the thought of having a warm place to go, "but, are you sure you can find your sister's home in this snow?"

"Oh easily," said Monroe. "Just follow me."

Then, with Monroe pulling the wagon and Warton pushing, they started off. Although

Monroe had said it was only a short way, it seemed to Warton that they were going on and on. "It must seem a long way because we're going so slowly," he thought. But then he noticed they were traveling under tall evergreens, giant maples, and spreading oaks.

"Monroe," he called. "Didn't you say your sister lived on the open hillside?"

"That's where she lives all right," Monroe shouted back.

"But we're in the forest," called Warton.

Monroe stopped in his tracks. He spun around. "I thought we should have been there by now."

"You know what that means," said Warton.

Monroe nodded. "It means," he said softly, "that now, we're *both* lost in this blizzard."

Warton and Monroe stood silently under a drooping evergreen bough. Warton was listening to the delicate, feathery sound the snowflakes made as they drifted through its branches, when he noticed tears in Monroe's eyes.

"Don't worry," said Warton. "We'll find shelter somewhere."

"It's not that," sniffed Monroe. "I just feel terrible because you tried to help me, and now you're lost in a blizzard on Christmas Eve . . . and it's all my fault."

"It's not your fault that you don't see well," said Warton.

At that, Monroe's face brightened up a bit. "That's right, Warton," he said. "I can't be blamed for that, can I?"

"Of course not," said Warton. "So you shouldn't blame yourself for our being lost."

"Hooray!" shouted Monroe. "It's not my fault at all."

Monroe was so relieved, he jumped into the air. He smashed into a branch just above him and sent a shower of snow all over himself and Warton. It knocked them onto their backs and they looked as if they had suddenly grown white beards. When they saw each other, they laughed till tears rolled down their cheeks.

When Warton could finally talk, he said, "We'd better find a safer place to stay."

Monroe, still holding his sides and laughing, nodded.

When Warton and Monroe stepped out from under the bough, they were shocked at how fast the snow was falling.

"Let's hope we can find shelter soon," said Warton. "Darkness will be coming early."

Then they moved on through the forest. The farther they went, the worse the blizzard became. The wind grew to a constant roar and whipped enormous trees about as if they were mere saplings. Monroe, pushing at the back of the wagon, feared that, at any moment, he would be swept away. Warton, pulling at the front, bowed his head against the gale and tried not to slip and fall.

All the while, the snow grew deeper. Finally, they could no longer push through it. Monroe fell exhausted across the back of the wagon, his teeth chattering uncontrollably in the intense cold. Warton, as tired as he had ever been, sank

slowly down onto the snow. As the cold settled upon him, he began to feel drowsy.

"I must not go to sleep," he thought. "If I do, I may never wake up again." But, try as he would, he could not keep his eyes open. He gave one last effort and opened them wide. Just then a gust of wind swept the snow away from in front of him. It was only for an instant, but long enough for Warton to see something that made his heart skip a beat.

"Monroe!" he called, "I think I see a shelter."

"Hoo . . . Hoo . . . Hooray!" stammered the shivering mole.

What Warton had seen was on a small slope. Now, with the snow again blowing in his eyes, he was not sure exactly where it was. Even worse, he was not sure he had seen anything at all.

It took all of their remaining strength to go a little way up the slope, and just as it became impossible to go any farther, Warton saw it again. Directly before them, partly covered with drifted snow, was the dark mouth of a cave. They pushed the wagon through the snow, until it rolled onto an earthen floor. Warton and Monroe staggered in after it and fell upon the ground. They lay in silence for some time.

All was dark within the cave except for the dim light at the entrance. And, as night was already spreading across the forest, that too was beginning to fade.

Monroe was the first to stir. "I'm afraid I wouldn't have lasted much longer out there," he said as he sat up.

"We found this shelter just in time," said Warton. Then, feeling more like himself again, he hopped up. "I think it would be a good idea to explore this place."

"Wait," said Monroe, "I have some candles in my wagon. I'll get them and come along."

Monroe began poking through his things. "Ah, here we are. Light this, Warton, and we'll see what this place looks like."

"I'd better not," said Warton, "this is your toothbrush."

"Well, that won't do," chuckled Monroe, searching again. This time, he came up with two small, white candles.

As soon as they were lit, Warton and Monroe started for the back of the cave. They moved slowly, taking one cautious step at a time. Warton was noticing the way their shadows danced on the stone ceiling, when Monroe warned, "Watch your step!"

Warton looked down and saw a huge, white bone lying on the dirt. He jumped over it, and decided to stay close to Monroe.

To the little toad and mole the cave seemed like an enormous cavern. When they reached the back, Warton let out a cry. "Look!" he pointed ahead. Before them were two openings that appeared to be smaller caves within the larger cave.

"I'm going to investigate this one," said Warton, peering into one of the openings.

"And I'll stand guard," said Monroe.

"Okay." Warton held the candle high and stepped through the opening. Instantly, he felt a coolness. Then a draft caught the candle's flame and nearly blew it out. When the flame settled down he saw that he was in a room filled with food. There were piles of red, green, and yellow apples. There were heaps of berries and dried fruits. Stacked along one wall were huge chunks of meat. Dried fish hung from the ceiling.

"What luck!" whispered Warton. "At least we won't be hungry." Then he noticed a large wooden barrel in the farthest corner. A curved dipper, fastened with a rope, dangled from its side.

"Now, what could that be?" thought Warton, going closer. He leaped up and grabbed the rope that was attached to the dipper. Then he pulled himself to the top of the barrel. Holding on tightly, he looked over the edge. "Hmm," he said, "it's filled with some kind of gooey stuff." He sniffed. "Smells sweet too." Cautiously he tasted it. "Why, this whole bar-

rel is filled with honey. Someone is storing
food here. I wonder who it is? One thing is certain," he said, looking around the room, "he
must eat like a bear."

Suddenly, Warton's mouth fell open. His
eyes filled with alarm. "*That's* who lives here,"
he cried... "it's a bear!" Warton jumped to the
floor and dashed through the doorway.

"Monroe!" he cried. "We're in a bear's den!"

But the big cave was empty, and Monroe was gone.

"Monroe!" called Warton frantically. "Where are you?"

There was no answer.

Then Warton saw candlelight coming from the other opening. He hopped over and whispered, "Monroe, are you in there?"

"Yes," came the reply. "And guess what I've found, a big pile of fur rugs."

With his candle held out before him, Warton stepped into the room. "Monroe," he cried, "that isn't a pile of fur rugs you're standing on . . . it's a bear!"

"Oh my goodness!" cried Monroe, trembling all over.

"Run!" whispered Warton. "Before he wakes up!"

The little mole was so frightened he couldn't move. "Oh my goodness!" he said again.

"Hurry!" warned Warton.

But Monroe was rooted to the bear's shoulder.

Warton hopped over to the bear and began to climb up towards Monroe. "Come on, Monroe!" he urged. "Hurry!"

Finally, Monroe took one nervous step towards Warton. But, when he did, he was trembling so much he dropped his candle.

"Oh no!" cried Warton as it landed behind the bear's ear.

There was a wisp of smoke and a small burst of flame. And Warton and Monroe went flying into the air as the bear sprang to his feet,

howling and jumping up and down on all fours. Then he stood up on two legs and danced about in wild circles.

At last, he stopped. From the middle of the room he looked all around until his eyes fell upon the terrified toad and mole.

"So, there you are," growled the bear. "I suppose you think it's a very funny thing for two pitiful creatures like you to set fire to a powerful and beautiful bear such as me."

"It was an accident," spoke up Warton.

"That's right," said Monroe. "I thought you were a fur rug."

"A fur rug!" snarled the bear. "What sort of an idiot would set fire to a fur rug?"

"He's not an idiot!" said Warton. "He just doesn't see well."

The bear lowered his head and stared into the mole's tiny eyes. "Too bad for you," he said. "Now, I see very well. I also hear and smell perfectly. Then the bear curled back his lips. "I also have perfect teeth."

Monroe swallowed hard and tugged at Warton's sleeve. "He's g . . . going to eat us!" he cried.

"Eat *you?*" laughed the bear. "Never! I eat only perfect foods — the purest honey, the sweetest berries, the choicest meats, and the plumpest fish. Now, just look at yourselves."

Warton and Monroe glanced nervously at each other.

"As you can see," sneered the bear, "neither one of you is perfect. In fact, you both look quite disgusting."

"I'm thankful for that," said Monroe.

"You can also be thankful that I am too tired to punish you," said the bear with a yawn. "I need at least eight more weeks of sleep. So, get out of my sleeping chamber, and don't bother me again!" He turned and waddled back to his pile of straw.

Warton and Monroe could not get out of the room fast enough, and they ran straight back to the wagon.

"Well," said Warton in hushed tones, "it looks as if we can stay here as long as we don't wake him up."

"Do you think so?" said Monroe. "Then I guess I'll unpack my wagon, before the snow melts and ruins my things."

Warton was happy to have something to do, so he pitched in with Monroe, and soon the wagon was empty.

When they were finished, they stood at the entrance of the cave, looking out. By now, it was completely dark outside and the snow was still falling.

"My sister and nephews and nieces must be waiting and waiting for me," said Monroe, sniffing a little. "This will be the first time I have not brought them a Christmas tree."

Warton was feeling just as bad. "This will be the first time I have not spent Christmas Eve with my brother Morton and Grampa Arbuckle. I know I've spoiled everything for them, too." Warton thought of how much he would miss their happy faces tonight, and, of course, his favorite part of Christmas Eve, the part that came at the very end.

They stood there a while longer. Then Warton and Monroe turned and looked at each other. And each was startled by how sad the other looked. At once, their sad thoughts seemed to vanish.

"Say," said Warton; "I've just remembered something I have in my pack. Let's have some hot chocolate and some delicious Christmas cookies."

"That sounds wonderful," said Monroe, feeling better already. "And, as long as I'm not going to get to my sister's tonight, why don't we set up the Christmas tree right here?"

Warton suddenly felt much better himself, and eagerly helped set up the little tree. Monroe found a few more candles, and they fastened them to some of the branches.

"I only wish we had some ornaments," said Monroe.

"Me too," said Warton. Then he blinked. "If we only had some string," he said, "we could use half of these cookies to decorate the tree. The other half we could eat."

Monroe ran to his wagon and held up a ball of string. Happily, they began hanging the cookies on the tree. There were buttercup crisps, spearmint squares, birchbark curls, and blueberry snaps, all made in different shapes. Some were sleighs, some were bells, others were Christmas trees and stars, and some were tiny cottages.

When they were done, Monroe spread a green tablecloth on the dirt floor. Warton poured the hot chocolate, and then divided the

remaining cookies. Just before they sat down, they lit all the candles on the Christmas tree. In the soft light, the cave seemed almost cozy.

Monroe was contentedly munching on one of the cookies when he noticed Warton blinking.

"I've just thought of something," said Warton. "I'll bet that grumpy old bear doesn't realize that this is Christmas Eve. If someone doesn't tel¹ him, he'll sleep right through."

"But, he didn't want to be disturbed," said Monroe.

"He probably doesn't realize this is Christmas Eve," said Warton. "I think I should tell him." He hopped up and went straight to the back of the cave. When he looked in, he saw the bear curled up and sleeping soundly.

Warton had forgotten how big he was, and, as he listened to the heavy breathing, he wondered if he should go in.

"Oh well," he thought, entering, "I'm sure he wants to know. He took a deep breath and tapped on the bear's nose. The bear didn't budge. Warton tapped again, this time as hard as he could. Still the bear didn't move.

"He's some sound sleeper," said Warton. Then he drew back his foot and kicked the bear in the nose.

The bear's eyes popped open, and he stared in astonishment at Warton. "You didn't just kick my nose, did you?"

"Yes I did," said Warton nervously. "I want to tell you something important."

"Important!" growled the bear as he sat up.

"It better be important — important enough to wake me from my sleep!"

"It is," said Warton. "Tonight is Christmas Eve!"

"What!" snarled the bear. "You mean you dared wake me just to tell me about a silly thing like Christmas?"

"Silly?" said Warton. "Christmas isn't silly."

The bear sneered, "To someone like me it is. It is definitely not a reason to waken me!" He sounded angrier all the tin. "Don't you know that Christmas is only three things — Christmas trees, Christmas food, and Christmas presents. To me that's silly!"

"But . . ." said Warton.

"Oh, you don't believe me?" roared the bear. "Then I'll show you." He stormed out of his sleeping chamber. Seeing Monroe sitting quietly by the Christmas tree, he charged at him.

Monroe nearly choked on a cookie. "I . . . I guess you're not glad to hear that it's Christmas Eve," he stammered.

The bear just glanced at Monroe. Then he picked up the Christmas tree, stomped to the entrance of the cave, and tossed it out.

Warton and Monroe watched, speechless, as the bear tramped out into the driving snow. They heard a thrashing about, and then the sound of splintering wood. Soon the bear stormed back into the cave, dragging a huge spruce tree. He grasped the trunk, and drove it into the earth.

"There," he said. "Isn't this a beautiful tree?"

Warton and Monroe both nodded.

"Of course it is," said the bear. "And I can get a tree like this any day of the year! Not just on Christmas Eve!"

Then he stood over the cookies and hot chocolate. He gave the tablecloth a kick that sent it flying across the cave. Then he lumbered back to his storeroom, returning with a large sack. He turned it upside down, and apples, berries, fruits, and meats scattered everywhere. "Also," said the bear, "I have a barrel of pure honey.

Now, isn't that a feast?"

Again, Warton and Monroe nodded.

"Of course it is," said the bear proudly. "And I can have a feast like that anytime, not just on Christmas Eve!"

Then the bear waddled over and stood glaring at Warton. "Now, there's one more thing, isn't there?" he said to the frightened toad. "Give me a present!"

"B . . . but I have nothing to give you," stammered Warton.

"Give me those ice skates!" demanded the bear.

Warton knew he had no choice, so he handed them over.

The bear turned to Monroe. "You're next!" he snapped.

Grabbing the first thing he saw, the trembling mole gave the bear his alarm clock.

"You see?" said the bear. "I can also get

presents whenever I want, not just on Christmas Eve." He threw the skates and alarm clock back at Warton and Monroe. "That was just to show you why Christmas is silly for someone like me." Then he stuffed all his food into the sack. As he started back towards his sleeping chamber he bellowed, "I can have all the things of Christmas whenever I want!"

"But you don't have any Christmas spirit," said Warton.

The bear spun around. "And, just what is that?" he snorted.

"I don't really know," said Warton. "I just know that you don't have any."

"Ha!" said the bear. "If you don't even know what it is, there's no such thing." Then, turning away he roared, "Just remember, don't dare disturb me again!"

As Monroe let out a sigh of relief, Warton said, "I wouldn't disturb him again for anything." He straightened out the crumpled tablecloth. "Look," he said, "we still have two cookies left."

"I'm going to look for some more candles," said Monroe.

But, in all the mole's belongings there was only one candle left. Monroe fastened it carefully to the lowest branch, and Warton hung one of the cookies next to it. They broke the other cookie into tiny pieces, and ate them slowly as they sat under the tree.

As they ate, Warton's eye fell upon Monroe's alarm clock. It was just after ten. He knew if he were home now, everyone would just be sitting down to Morton's delicious meal. After that, the presents would be opened, and he would wait eagerly for midnight and his favorite part of Christmas Eve. Then Warton wondered if he and Monroe would ever get home. Even if the snow stopped, they had no way to get through it. And they wouldn't know which way to go anyway.

These thoughts weighed heavily on Warton's mind, and he decided he would just have to think of something more cheerful. Soon he was chuckling softly.

"Are you telling yourself jokes?" asked Monroe.

"Oh no," replied Warton. "I was thinking of last Christmas Eve. We had just finished eating, when my brother Morton said he felt like some cheese and jelly. But Grampa Arbuckle thought he said he had fleas on his belly. So he threw flea powder all over him. Morton was so surprised, he knocked the gravy boat onto Grampa's toe. Then Grampa started yelling, and, because of the flea powder, Morton and I started sneezing. It was some mix-up!" chortled Warton.

"If you think that was a mix-up," snickered Monroe, "you should come to my sister's house." He swallowed the last of the cookie crumbs. "You see, my sister Matilda has always loved the name Clarence. So naturally, when her first baby was born, she named him Clarence. But when it came time to name her second, she just couldn't bring herself to give him any other name. So she named that one Clarence, too," Monroe sighed. "Now she has twelve boys named Clarence and eleven girls named Clara. Believe me, it's very confusing there."

Warton laughed at the thought of it.

They grew quiet as they remembered other Christmases, spent with their loved ones in the snug safety of their own homes, instead of in a big cave, in a howling blizzard.

Warton leaned against the tree and began to hum his favorite Christmas carol, "Oh Joyful Night." Monroe sat on his wagon and joined in. Then they sang "The Brightest Star," which was Monroe's favorite. They sang quietly at first, but, by the time they got to "The Light on the Christmas Rose," they were singing more and more loudly. Their voices blended beautifully, and they were enjoying themselves so much they didn't realize that every note echoed loudly through the cave. As they started the second verse of "Listen to the Chimes," the tree began to shake.

Warton peered out from underneath. His heart chilled when he saw the bear glaring down at him.

"I thought I told you not to disturb me," snarled the bear.

"I'm sorry," choked Warton. "We didn't realize how loudly we were singing."

"Is that right?" snorted the bear. "Well, now you can sing as loudly as you want . . . somewhere else! I want you to leave."

"But it's snowing!" cried Warton. "It's snowing hard."

"We could never get through it," cried Monroe.

"Isn't that too bad!" said the bear.

Warton and Monroe were stunned. They looked at the bear. His nostrils were flaring, his eyes were dark, and his lips were curled back. Nowhere on his face could they see the slightest sign of forgiving.

With a sigh, Warton helped Monroe load his wagon. Then they bundled up once again in their heavy clothes. After Warton put on his pack, they were ready to go.

At the entrance of the cave, they looked out into the blackness, and they heard the wind howl as it swept icy snow against their faces. They glanced back at the bear, who waited impatiently for them to leave. Then they stepped out into the raging blizzard.

As soon as Warton and Monroe left the cave, the storm pounced upon them. The snow found its way through the tiniest openings in their clothing. The wind sucked the very breath from their mouths.

They had gone but a few steps when the wagon overturned, and it and Warton and Monroe tumbled down the slope.

The wagon rolled against a rock, and Warton rolled against the wagon. He got up slowly, and, some distance away, he saw Monroe also getting up. But then Monroe started trudging off . . . in the opposite direction.

"Monroe!" cried Warton. "This way!"

"I'm going to look for my Christmas tree," called Monroe, "just in case we get home alive." Then he was swallowed up in a cloud of blowing snow.

Warton was horrified. He started after

Monroe but he could scarcely move through the snow, and there were too many places to look.

"I must do something soon," he thought, "before it's too late." Then he shook his head. "But what can I do? I'm too small to get through this snow." His eyes narrowed. "But I do know someone who isn't small. But *he* would never help. Still this *is* Christmas Eve, and perhaps, just perhaps, he might."

Pushing, and digging, and shoving, he made his way back up the slope to the bear's cave.

Once inside, he hurried to the bear's chamber. The sleeping bear was curled up on the straw, a smile on his face.

"Oh, oh," thought Warton, "he's probably having a dream about blueberry fields on a summer day. When he wakes up and sees me here, he'll be angrier than ever." Warton swallowed nervously. "I must try," he told himself. He took a deep breath and kicked the bear sharply on the end of his nose.

The bear opened his eyes and blinked.

"Thank goodness I was able to awaken you," said Warton.

Slowly the bear rolled out of the straw. He took three deliberate steps and put his nose directly against Warton's frightened face. "Why shouldn't you be able to awaken me?" he said, breathing hard. "You've had enough practice!"

Warton gulped. "I'm sorry," he said, "but something terrible has happened. Monroe went off to look for his Christmas tree. I'm sure he's lost by now."

"Who cares?" said the bear. "Just tell me why you woke me!"

"Will you help me find him?" said Warton. "Please?"

"What!" roared the bear. "Haven't I told you I need my sleep, and haven't I told you not to bother me again?" The bear's chest was heaving. "Now, once and for all, get out!"

Warton ran through the doorway. But, just on the other side, he stopped. Although he feared for his life, he knew there was one more thing he had to say. He stepped inside.

The bear was sitting with his back against the wall. His arms were hanging down and his eyes were blinking.

"Pardon me," said Warton, his voice tight with fear, "if, by any chance, Monroe should come in here, please tell him to wait, and I will look in every so often."

"What!" cried the bear. "Will I *never* see the last of you two? Will I *never* get any sleep?" Then he groaned. "Why aren't you both home where you belong anyway?"

"I wish we were," said Warton. Then, noticing the bear grinding his teeth, he spun around and hopped out of the room. He dashed through the cave and was getting ready to step outside when he heard a commotion. He looked back and saw the bear bursting out of his chamber doorway. The bear stood a moment, looking about with a wild expression. Then, giving a roar, he made straight for Warton.

Warton felt as if his legs had turned to jelly. His eyes darted about but he saw no place to hide.

Without stopping, the bear scooped him up and rushed out into the storm.

Warton shouted, "I'm sorry I awakened you. I promise I'll never do it again!"

"That's right!" roared the bear. "I'm going to make sure of that!"

"Wh . . . what are you going to do?" gasped Warton.

"I'm doing the only thing possible so that I can get some sleep," growled the bear. "I'm taking you and your near-sighted friend to wherever you live so I'll be rid of you once and for all. Then I'm coming back to my bed to get some sleep. Now, what's your friend's name?"

Warton was so relieved and delighted, he could hardly speak. "It's Monroe," he said finally.

"MONROE!" called the bear. His gruff voice carried like a foghorn through the forest. "MONROE!" The bear plowed through the snow, tearing up bushes and uprooting small trees, all the while shouting, "MONROE! MONROE!"

There was no answer.

Then it occurred to Warton that Monroe would never answer — not to a bear. Not wanting to offend the bear, he wondered what to do. Then he took a deep breath, and started to yodel.

The bear could hardly believe his ears, and he snapped his head around. "Are you gargling?" he asked in amazement.

"I'm yodeling," replied Warton.

The bear shook his head as Warton let out another yodel.

"I'm over here," came Monroe's voice.

The bear lunged into a thicket of laurel bushes. There, Monroe was trying to free his Christmas tree from a low branch.

"Oh good," cried Warton. "You've found your Christmas tree."

"Yes," replied Monroe, too busy to look up. "But speak softly. That miserable bear is out here in the woods looking for us."

"That's right," growled the bear. "And now I've found you."

Monroe was so shocked, he let go of the tree and fell over backwards. "Oh my goodness!" he cried.

Roughly, the bear picked up Monroe and his tree, and set them on his back.

"Don't worry," said Warton. "He's going to take both of us right to our homes so he can get some sleep."

"He is?" cried Monroe. "What a wonderful present!"

"It's a present all right," grunted the bear as he pushed through the laurel bushes. "It's a present for *me*."

When Warton pointed out the wagon, the bear tossed it onto his back without even stopping. Warton and Monroe tied the tree to the wagon as best they could as the bear lumbered along.

"Monroe's sister lives at the top of the hillside overlooking the pond," shouted Warton, "and I live under the twin hemlocks a short way up the wide path."

The bear just grunted. Unlike Warton and Monroe, he traveled in nearly a straight line. So, what to them was a long journey, to the bear was nothing at all. He pushed his way through bushes and stepped over fallen logs. When he came to a stream, he splashed right through it. Many times, Warton and Monroe would have been thrown off if they hadn't held on tightly.

Even so, Warton was beginning to enjoy himself. "I've never b . . . b . . . been on a b . . . bear ride before," he said as he bounced about.

"M . . . m . . . me neither," said Monroe.

As the bear plowed steadily through the

drifting snow, Warton and Monroe became so happy at the prospect of being home for Christmas, they began to sing "Merry, Merry Lingonberry."

"Say," shouted Warton to the bear, "why don't you sing too?"

"Be quiet!" snapped the bear. "Just be quiet!"

Warton looked at Monroe and they stopped singing.

A bit later, as they were passing beneath some tall hickory trees, they heard a faint whimpering. The bear stopped and poked his snout about in the snow. "Huh," he grunted. "So that's all it is." Then he continued on his way.

"What was it?" asked Warton.

"Just a baby squirrel," said the bear.

Warton was shocked. "Stop!" he cried. "We can't leave that baby squirrel there."

"We can't?" sneered the bear. "Of course we can." And he started off.

"Well, I'm going to jump off," said Warton, "and try to help that little squirrel."

"Me too." Monroe pushed his wagon off into the snow. Then he and Warton jumped after it.

The bear looked astonished. "Well, the three of you will freeze now," he said with a shrug. Then he started back to his cave.

Warton and Monroe were too busy to pay any attention. When they got to the little squirrel, they brushed away as much of the snow as they could.

"Look how he's shivering," said Warton. "We must find a way to get him back up to his home."

"But, how can we get him up the tree?" said Monroe.

"Give him to me!" ordered a gruff voice.

Warton and Monroe were startled to see the bear behind them.

"I had a terrible thought," growled the bear. "We're still too close to my cave. I don't know how, but I just know you two will find your way back there, and you'll probably have the squirrel with you this time."

The bear snatched the little squirrel out of the snow. Holding it in his mouth, he put his paws around the tree, and began climbing, grumbling all the way. When he reached the only squirrel home he could see, he tapped on the door.

A mother squirrel stepped out. "Oh!" she shrieked, about to run back inside.

"Is this yours?" growled the bear.

"My baby!" screamed the mother squirrel. "I thought he was in bed. He must have gotten up to watch the snow and fallen out."

"Well, take him!" ordered the bear, handing

over the baby squirrel.

"Wait!" cried the mother squirrel. "Please wait." And she disappeared inside her home.

"I don't wait for anyone," snarled the bear. He shook his head and was about to back down the tree, but the mother squirrel was already back. This time the father squirrel was with her.

"There's no way we can thank you enough,"

said the father. "But, at least, we'd like to give you a small gift."

"A gift?" said the bear.

"It's a package of the finest nuts that grow in the forest. We know it's not much, for someone like you, but we'd be happy if you would accept it."

"A gift?" said the bear again. "For someone like me? Well . . . all right, I'll take it."

As he started backing down the tree, the mother squirrel called after him, "Merry Christmas!"

"Merry Christmas," mumbled the bear. He was halfway down the tree before he realized what he had said. He stopped, looked up, shook his head in surprise, then continued downward.

"It looks like it's going to be a lovely night after all," said Warton.

"What's that supposed to mean?" said the bear.

"Look," said Monroe. "It's almost stopped snowing."

The bear looked up, and, sure enough, only a few scattered flakes were drifting downward.

Warton, seeing the small package the bear was holding, asked, "What's that, a Christmas present?"

"This?" growled the bear. "It's nothing! I'll probably throw it away."

But Warton noticed that, instead of throwing it away, he seemed to hold the package a little more tightly.

Then the bear growled, "Now, get on my back, you two. I haven't got all night!"

As Warton and Monroe climbed aboard, the moon came out, and everywhere, the new fallen snow glistened under its silvery light.

"I've never seen the forest more beautiful," said Warton.

"It will be even more beautiful when I get rid of you two," said the bear.

For a while, no one spoke. Then, as they were passing a clearing in the middle of a pine grove, they saw a strange sight — hundreds of white rabbits, all facing in the same direction,

not one of them making a sound.

The bear paid no attention but just plodded on.

Warton looked at Monroe. "I didn't know that rabbits gathered like that on Christmas Eve, did you?"

Monroe shook his head.

Then Warton shouted to the bear, "Did you know about that?"

But the bear was holding the squirrels' little gift so tightly in his mouth that he couldn't answer.

Soon they came to the open field on the hillside, and Warton could see the pond below. The ice he had skated on that morning was now under a thick blanket of snow. He thought sadly about how he had wanted the time to pass quickly then. Now, he wished time would stop so he could get home for at least the last part of Christmas Eve. "It must be nearly midnight now," he thought, "and we still have a way to go."

Following the woodline at the top of the hillside, the bear came to the home of Monroe's sister. The entrance was between two large stones and was nearly free of snow.

"Well," growled the bear, stopping near the door, "do I have to wait all winter for you to get off?"

"Oh no," cried Monroe. He said goodbye to Warton, and then jumped off. "I hope we meet again sometime."

"Me too," said Warton as the bear started off.

Suddenly, Monroe let out a cry, "Oh my

goodness! I've forgotten my wagon!"

The bear stopped and looked back at Warton. "Well, push it off," he snapped. "I don't want to carry it around all night."

"All right," said Warton. He was about to give the wagon a shove, when a shaft of yellow light fell upon him. He blinked and saw that the door of the little home was open, and Matilda the mole was rushing out.

"Monroe," she cried as she hugged him, "is it really you? How did you ever get through all that snow?"

"He brought me," said Monroe, pointing.

Matilda turned around and nearly fainted. When she could speak, she said, "Monroe! That's a bear!"

"I know," said Monroe. "And that toad on his back is my friend Warton."

"I'm pleased to meet you," said Matilda.

Just then little moles began streaming out of the doorway. One by one they came, till all twelve Clarences and eleven Claras were running happily around Monroe. "Did you bring the Christmas tree? they cried.

The bear, growing very impatient, grabbed the wagon off his back and dropped it in the snow. "Here!" he snorted.

At first the children were afraid of the big bear and his loud voice. But when they saw the Christmas tree they quickly forgot their fright and went to look at it.

"Oh, it's beautiful, it's perfect, it's wonderful!" cried all the Claras and Clarences.

The bear looked astonished at the fuss they were making over the scraggly, little tree.

Matilda stood close to Monroe and watched as her children ran joyfully around the wagon. Then she went over to the bear. "Oh dear, oh dear," she said, looking up at him.

"It's a pitiful tree all right," said the bear.

"Oh no," said Matilda, "it's beautiful. My children just love it. And we are all so grateful to you for bringing my brother Monroe safely through the storm. I wish I could invite you in, but you wouldn't fit. And I have no present at all that I could give someone like you. Oh dear."

Suddenly, Matilda jumped up and kissed the bear on his nose. "Thank you," she said, "and Merry Christmas!"

The bear's legs began to wobble. He was so flabbergasted he replied with the only thing he could think of, "Merry Christmas!"

Then the little moles began running around the bear. "Merry Christmas!" they shouted.

Once again, the bear could hardly believe what he had said. He stood a few moments, twitched his nose, and started off.

Warton waved to Monroe and the others. Then he settled back and listened to the crunch of snow under the bear's feet. "It must be nearly midnight," he thought. "If only he would run, I might still get home in time for my favorite part of Christmas Eve." Warton was wondering if he dared ask when he realized with horror that the bear was walking even more slowly than before. "Are you all right?" asked Warton.

"If you must know," snapped the bear, "I'm very sleepy."

Warton knew he would not get home in time now.

They were nearly at the place where the wide path led up into the forest. The bear was plodding along, going more slowly all the time, when there came the sound of tiny bells. Their delicate tones were brilliantly clear on the crisp night air.

"I wonder what that could be," whispered Warton.

Then they came to the path — the path that

led into the forest and to Warton's home. The bells were much louder now. Warton looked ahead, and caught his breath. His eyes opened wide. For, part way up the path, the very snow itself seemed to be exploding. Here and there puffs of snow shot into the air, and with each puff there came the tinkle of bells.

Warton could not take his eyes off the fantastic sight. The bear began to growl, deep down in his throat. The exploding snow moved straight down the wide path, coming closer and closer. The bear stood up high on his hind legs, snarling at the snow as Warton held on for dear life.

Then the snow exploded directly in front of the bear. And Warton let out a yell. "Morton! It's Morton!"

There was another puff and Morton burst out of the snow. His feet were firmly attached to the pedals of a pogo stick, and he had a large pack on his back. From a belt around his middle, there hung a row of tiny bells.

Then there was another burst of snow, and

Grampa Arbuckle popped up beside Morton. Then Sebastian the field mouse shot out of the snow.

All three were outfitted the same, except that Sebastian had an extra long muffler wrapped around his tail.

Warton was overjoyed, and he jumped off the bear's back to embrace his three rescuers.

"Warton! Thank goodness you're safe!" said Morton, glancing nervously at the bear. "We were worried sick, and not being able to go looking for you made it even worse."

Then Grampa Arbuckle, who was huffing and puffing quite a bit, said, "Sebastian and I got to talking about the days when we used to race together in cross-country pogo sticking. I dug these 'sticks' out of my closet, and here we are."

"The bells were my idea," said Sebastian, "so you'd hear us coming."

Warton was so happy, he could hardly speak. But then, suddenly, he looked glum. "I wish I hadn't spoiled Christmas Eve for everyone."

"Nonsense!" said Grampa. "It can't be spoiled if everyone's all right." Then Grampa adjusted his spectacles. "You *are* all right, aren't you?" he said, squinting at the bear, and then at Warton.

"Oh yes," said Warton. "Although I must admit, at times I was worried. That is, until this bear said he was going to bring me home. And, except for when he stopped to return a baby squirrel to its parents, and to take a mole with a Christmas tree to where he was going, he brought me straight here."

They all looked at the sleepy bear whose head was drooping lower and lower, his eyes nearly shut.

Then Morton hopped close to the bear. He looked up, and, with admiration in his eyes, he said, "You needn't take Warton any farther because we have a pogo stick for him, too. And, if I may say so, I think it's a wonderful thing that there are those like you who take the time to help others. I'm honored to meet you."

"That goes for me too," said Grampa Arbuckle.

"What a prince!" said Sebastian.

The bear, who was so sleepy he hardly knew where he was, just grunted. Then he started walking away.

"Wait!" cried Morton. "You must wait!"

"I must wait?" mumbled the bear.

"Please!" said Morton. "We have lots of food in our packs, in fact, everything we need for our Christmas Eve feast."

Warton's eyes opened wide at that.

"Won't you please share it with us?" continued Morton. "It's the only way we can show our appreciation."

The bear opened his tired eyes a bit. He

looked at Morton's admiring face. "Well, I am a little hungry," he said, turning slowly around.

Morton, Grampa, and Sebastian were delighted.

And Warton could not believe he had not missed the Christmas Eve feast after all. After the packs were unloaded, he helped Morton spread a large red tablecloth on the snow. One by one, all the things of the Christmas Eve feast were set upon it, from the roast jumbo crayfish and mashed potato bugs to the white fly pie and elderberry tea.

Then everyone sat down to eat. Even though the moon was shining brightly, Morton lit the Christmas candles. Then Grampa carved the crayfish in thick, juicy slices. The plates were passed to Morton, and he put a little of everything on each one. For the bear, he filled two plates till they overflowed.

"Mmm, mmm," said Warton as the feasting began, "you've done it again, Morton!"

"He's some cook!" said Grampa.

"Fine food, just fine!" said Sebastian. After

they had been eating for some time, the field mouse began to cackle. "You toads are something," he said. "Who else would have a picnic on the snow?"

Warton chuckled, and looked to see if the bear thought it was funny too. But the bear was busy eating. "That's odd," thought Warton. "I know Morton gave him the biggest portions, but still, they must be the tiniest of tastes to him." It almost seemed to Warton that the bear was pretending the little morsels were more than enough.

As Warton was reaching for a slice of crayfish, he noticed that his brother was shivering from the cold. But he could tell from the look of sheer pleasure on Morton's face that he didn't even know it.

When the other food finally disappeared, Morton placed a piece of pie and a cup of tea before everyone. He gave three pieces to the bear.

As soon as the pie was finished, Grampa Arbuckle stood up. He took out his watch, stud-

ied it, and put it back. Then he cleared his
throat. "Midnight passed long ago," he said,
"but it really doesn't matter. So I will now tell
the Christmas story that I tell every year."

Happily Warton settled down for his favorite part of Christmas Eve. As Grampa Arbuckle began, he noticed that only one small
cloud remained in the star-filled sky. He listened carefully as Grampa Arbuckle told the
story exactly as he had every year that Warton
could remember, and he wondered if perhaps
one year, a long time from now, he would be
telling the story himself.

And just as it had happened every year before, a strange and wonderful feeling stole over him. And it seemed as if the stars twinkled more and more brightly as the story went on.

Then Grampa Arbuckle was finished.

For a while, everyone was silent. Then Sebastian said, "That's a beautiful story."

Warton and Morton nodded.

Then it was time to leave. As they began to pick up their things, they noticed the bear had gone.

"I didn't even see him leave," said Morton.

"I know he was anxious to get home," said Warton.

One by one, everything went back into the packs — the plates and silverware, the dirty cups, the empty bowls and the half melted candles. And as Warton folded the tablecloth, he decided he had never had a finer Christmas Eve.

They all mounted their pogo sticks and started up the path towards home. As they

hopped along, Warton began having visions of
the warm little bed that awaited him.

Suddenly, Grampa Arbuckle stopped.
"What's that?" he said.

The others stopped and listened. But they
heard only the sound of the fir trees rustling
overhead. Then, from somewhere far off in the
forest, they heard what sounded like the wind
blowing through a hollow log.

95

"Could that be someone singing?" asked Sebastian.

Then the fir trees stopped their rustling, and they all heard it clearly. Someone with a gruff, powerful voice was drowsily singing, "Merry, Merry Lingonberry."

"My," said Morton, "that bear certainly has the Christmas Spirit."

Warton blinked in surprise. "He does, doesn't he?" he said.